The Bat Sprites

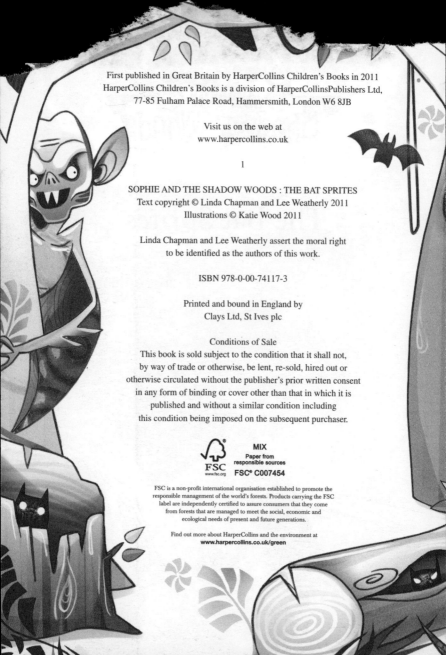

First published in Great Britain by HarperCollins Children's Books in 2011
HarperCollins Children's Books is a division of HarperCollinsPublishers Ltd,
77-85 Fulham Palace Road, Hammersmith, London W6 8JB

Visit us on the web at
www.harpercollins.co.uk

1

SOPHIE AND THE SHADOW WOODS : THE BAT SPRITES
Text copyright © Linda Chapman and Lee Weatherly 2011
Illustrations © Katie Wood 2011

Linda Chapman and Lee Weatherly assert the moral right
to be identified as the authors of this work.

ISBN 978-0-00-74117-3

Printed and bound in England by
Clays Ltd, St Ives plc

MIX
Paper from
responsible sources
FSC® C007454

FSC is a non-profit international organisation established to promote the
responsible management of the world's forests. Products carrying the FSC
label are independently certified to assure consumers that they come
from forests that are managed to meet the social, economic and
ecological needs of present and future generations.

Find out more about HarperCollins and the environment at
www.harpercollins.co.uk/green

More

adventures:

Linda Chapman & Lee Weatherly

The Bat Sprites

Northumberland County Council	
3 0132 02094874 6	
Askews & Holts	Feb-2012
JF	£4.99

Illustrated by Katie Wood

HarperCollins *Children's Books*

To all the team at HarperCollins for bringing Sophie so wonderfully to life. In particular, thank you to Ann-Janine Murtagh for being so keen on a heroine like Sophie in the first place, to Elorine Grant for the wonderful design of the books, Katie Woods for her fantastic illustrations and to our brilliant editors, Harriet Wilson and Rose Harrow for all their great thoughts and ideas.

Thank you!

Contents

The Shadow Woods

Very few people ever enter the Shadow Woods. The crooked trees press closely together, their branches reaching out like skeletons' arms. Strange whispers echo through the quiet air, and eyes seem to watch from the shadows. Anyone who does go in soon leaves, their skin prickling with fear. For these woods are like no others. Hidden deep within them is a gateway to the Shadow Realm – a dark and chaotic world where all the mischief-making creatures like goblins, boggles and trolls live.

Many hundreds of years ago, the Shadow Realm

creatures could pass freely between our world and theirs, but they caused so much trouble that it was decided the gateway between the two worlds must be shut for good. Yet no one knew how to do this, until a locksmith with magical powers made an iron key and then slotted a gem from the Shadow Realm into its handle. The secret had been found! The locksmith forced as many shadow creatures as he could back into their own world and locked the gateway firmly behind them.

From that day on, the locksmith became the Guardian of the Gateway, watching over the precious key and stopping the few shadow creatures left in this world from causing too much trouble. As he grew old he passed his powers on to

his grandson, who in turn passed the powers on to his. For hundreds of years, the Guardianship has passed down from grandparent to grandchild, and the gate has always remained safely shut.

But now for the first time, disaster looms. The shadow creatures have stolen the iron key! Luckily, there was no gem in its handle when it was taken, but there are six gems from the Shadow Realm hidden somewhere in our world. If the shadow creatures find any of them, they'll be able to slot them into the key and open the gateway, letting hordes of villainous creatures loose to cause mayhem and trouble.

Only one girl stands in their way… and her name is Sophie Smith.

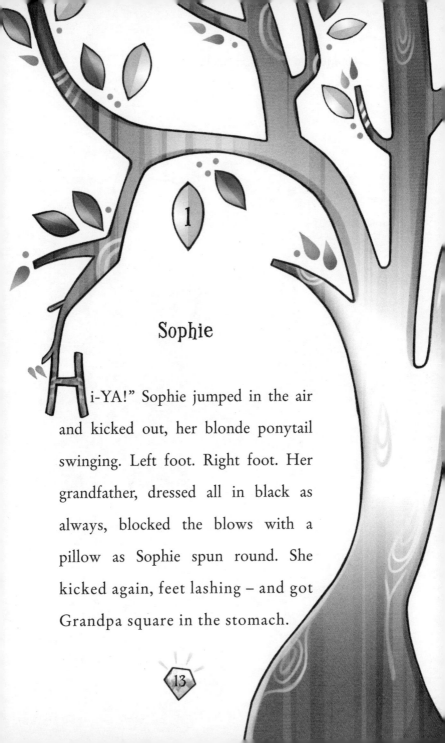

1

Sophie

"Hi-YA!" Sophie jumped in the air and kicked out, her blonde ponytail swinging. Left foot. Right foot. Her grandfather, dressed all in black as always, blocked the blows with a pillow as Sophie spun round. She kicked again, feet lashing – and got Grandpa square in the stomach.

"Ooof!" He staggered backwards, dropping the pillow.

Sophie stopped in alarm. "Grandpa! Are you OK?"

14

Her grandfather rested his hands on his knees, drawing in a deep breath. "I'm fine. You just caught me by surprise. Good – very good, child."

Sophie pushed her fringe back. "I'm getting better at fighting, aren't I?"

"Much better," Grandpa agreed. "However, you must continue to hone your fighting skills…"

As he talked, Sophie caught sight of herself in his bedroom mirror and admired her new green t-shirt with a picture of an electric guitar on it. Her mum and dad had sent it to her and it had arrived that morning.

"You must focus, concentrate and…" Grandpa's voice turned stern. "Sophie, are you listening to me?"

Sophie jumped guiltily. "Of course! I must practise, focus and concentrate. I must work night and day like you did when you were a young guardian. Oh, and I must always expect the unexpected," she said, ticking the points off on her fingers. It was easy to guess what Grandpa had been saying; he always said the same things.

Grandpa gave a slight frown. "Yes, exactly. You mustn't underestimate King Ug. He's cunning and dangerous, and now he has the key, he'll stop at nothing to open the gateway. There's no telling what creatures he'll send next!"

Sophie knew her grandpa was right. So far, King Ug had sent Swamp Boggles, Spider Gnomes, Fog Boggarts and Icicle Imps to help him find the gems he needed. Nervousness fluttered through her, but she pushed it away.

"Maybe it'll be fairy rabbits next," she suggested. "That'd be good."

"Sophie!" Grandpa snapped. "Please take this more seriously or you could get hurt. Now, let's get on with the practising."

"Grandpa..." Sophie paused as a thought struck her. "If I did get hurt – I mean really hurt, like being-dead-hurt... who would be the Guardian next?"

"Well, as you know, the Guardianship usually passes down from grandparent to grandchild," Grandpa replied. "But when there's no grandchild, the Guardian's closest blood relative becomes the next Guardian. There must always be a Guardian in our world, so if a Guardian dies, a new one will always be created. However," he fixed her with a look, "you are not going to die."

"Is that an order?" Sophie spoke lightly, though inside she felt her stomach clench.

"Yes," Grandpa replied softly. "It is." Their eyes met and Grandpa sighed. "Sophie, we both know I wasn't over the moon when you became the first girl Guardian, but you've proved me wrong. No Guardian could be braver and I'm very proud of you."

Surprise and pleasure warmed Sophie. She'd never have believed that she'd hear Grandpa say that, not in a million years!

"You're also my granddaughter and I'm determined that nothing bad is going happen to you," he went on. "Which is why," he held up his pillow, "we're going to practise some more!"

As Sophie and Grandpa practised, neither of them looked out the window. If they had, they might have noticed a figure that stood

near the woods, staring towards the house.

It was holding a key that glowed…

Later that evening, deep in the heart of the Shadow Woods, King Ug, the leader of the Ink Cap Goblins, paced around his toadstool clearing. His white, crumbly skin was covered with black blotches that oozed poisonous goo.

He looked up with a scowl as a goblin with a nose like a potato came scrambling through the trees.

"Well?" King Ug demanded. "Did you find one?"

"Yes, Your Majesty!" cried Potato Nose, triumphantly pulling something from his pocket.

King Ug stared at the small black creature that Potato Nose was holding. "Potato Nose – that is a bat."

"Yes, King Ug!" Potato Nose said eagerly.

"Did I or did I not ask for a Bat Sprite?"

"You did, King Ug!"

"So, Potato Nose, where is the sprite bit of that bat?"

"Um, it's… um… well… OW!" Potato Nose yelled as King Ug thwacked him.

"Fungus brain!" King Ug thundered as the bat flew away.

"King Ug! We've got one, we've got a sprite!" yelled two more goblins as they galloped into the clearing. One had a very flaky face and one had very large feet. Big Feet brandished something at the king. It looked like a small frog except that it had fangs and fingers and toes instead of webbed feet.

"Ribbit!" it croaked as it glared at King Ug.

"Oh, give me strength!" King Ug groaned. "That's not a Bat Sprite, it's a Frog Sprite! You lot have brains the size of peas! Tell me, what do you have?"

"Brains the size of peas," muttered the goblins, staring at the ground. The Frog Sprite hopped huffily away, pausing to kick Big Feet's ankle before it left.

"Don't you understand how important this is?" shouted King Ug. "There's just one more gem left to find! One last chance of opening the gateway! I need shadow creatures who are vicious and strong. I need large, evil, foul-smelling sprites…"

A bat flew into the clearing. As it swooped down, a ripple ran through it, and it changed into a figure slightly smaller than King Ug. "Like a

Bat Sprite, you mean?" it screeched as it landed.

"Erp!" King Ug squawked.

The Bat Sprite had a thin body covered with grey fur, with large bony hands, red eyes and wide black wings. "My family and I are the most vicious, evil and foul-smelling shadow creatures in this whole wood!" The Bat Sprite's voice squealed like a wet finger sliding down glass.

"So, King Ug, I hear you want our help opening the gateway?"

Trying not to make a face at the smell, King Ug cleared his throat and puffed out his chest. "Yes… er… yes, I do. The key glows whenever it's near a gem, and I've noticed it glowing near the Guardian's house. I believe the final gem is in there. Find it and bring it to me – then I'll open the gateway and we shadow creatures shall once more rule the world!"

The Bat Sprite nodded. "We shall do it!"

King Ug looked suddenly wary. "The Guardian is strong, you know. She'll try to stop you."

The Bat Sprite gave a shrieking laugh and showed its pointed fangs. "Then I promise you, she will be very sorry indeed!"

The Clue

Back at Keeper's Cottage, Sophie had just come to the end of her training session. "We must try to find the last hidden gem," Grandpa said, as he put the pillow back on his bed. "Have you got the other gems safe, Sophie?"

Sophie patted the purse belt

she always wore under her clothes. The five shadow gems that she and Sam had found so far clinked together inside the leather pouch. "Yes, they're here," she said.

"Good. There must be a clue to the whereabouts of the sixth gem in the Shadow Files somewhere. Keep searching for it." The turquoise gem was the only gem they hadn't yet found, and they knew that King Ug would do everything in his power to find it before they did.

"Already on to it." Sophie went to the door. "Book Boy!" she shouted.

Sam's red head popped out of her bedroom further down the landing. "Yep?"

Sam was Sophie's best friend. He was the only person in the world apart from

Grandpa who knew that Sophie was the Guardian, and he'd helped her in every one of her adventures so far. Grandpa hadn't been keen on him knowing at first, but Sam had proved to be very helpful. He loved reading and researching and was just as brave as Sophie.

"Any luck finding the final clue?" Sophie asked.

Shaking his head, Sam came to Grandpa's room, bringing an old leather-bound notebook with him – the Shadow Files. Over the years, all the previous Guardians had written notes in it about the creatures they'd faced. The Shadow Files also had clues to the hiding places of the six shadow gems. When each new Guardian took over, the gems magically moved to new hiding places and new clues would then appear in the book.

"No sign of the last clue yet," said Sam, flipping through the pages.

"We have to find it," said Grandpa. "It's absolutely essential! Once we get the final gem then we can hide them all somewhere safe, and try to get the key back. We must not fail! You're staying here tonight, aren't you, Sam?"

Sam nodded.

"We can talk more later then," said Grandpa. "I'm going out for a run."

"Should we go down to the kitchen?" Sophie said to Sam after Grandpa had gone. "I've been trying to teach Nigel to fetch. Come and see."

"Cool," said Sam.

Sophie grabbed her black fishing waistcoat from the bed and they headed downstairs.

Ten minutes later, Sophie pointed to the spoon she'd put on the table. "Go on. Fetch!" She tempted the parrot with a nut. "Then you can have this."

Nigel the parrot swooped to the table, picked up the spoon and flew back. He dropped it on the worktop beside Sophie, then landed on her shoulder and clicked his beak hopefully.

Sophie was delighted. "Good boy! You did it!" She stroked his feathers. "What a clever parrot."

"Gimme a carrot!" Nigel said, bobbing his head. He was very good at talking, though he often got the words wrong.

Sophie grinned. "I haven't got any carrots, but you can have a nut."

"Big butt!" Nigel replied, affectionately nuzzling her cheek.

Sophie giggled and glanced at Sam who was sitting at the table. He had started reading the Shadow Files again. "Did you see Nigel? He fetched the spoon!"

"YAY!" Sam leapt to his feet.

Sophie blinked. "Well, OK, I know it's good, but…"

"I've found the clue! Soph, look!" Sam's blue eyes shone as he jabbed his finger at the Shadow Files.

Sophie ran over. On a page about King Cobra Goblins, four tiny lines were written near the bottom in slanting, curly writing:

Hidden near where the Guardian sleeps

Search for a board that doth creak

Lift it up and you shall see

A gem shining beautifully.

Sophie gasped. "It *is* the clue! Oh, wow! We can start trying to find the gem right now."

"And it sounds like it might be easy. Look at

the first line," said Sam. "Hidden near where the Guardian sleeps. That must mean the turquoise gem is in this house!"

"I wonder what that bit about a board doth creak means?" said Sophie, puzzled.

"A floorboard, I bet. Have you got any creaky ones?" asked Sam.

"Not that I know of. Hang on – look! What's that?" Sophie pointed to a few other faint lines of text at the other side of the page. "Is that more of the clue?"

She read it out:

"If the goblin king joins gem and key

And opens the door then soon you'll see

There's no point fighting, it's too late

One Guardian will never close the gate."

Sophie and Sam stared uneasily at each other.

"I don't like the sound of that!" said Sam. "If you can't shut the gateway once it's opened, then we'd better make sure that it's never, ever opened!"

"We'd really better find that sixth gem before the shadow creatures do!" agreed Sophie, jumping to her feet.

There was the sound of a key in the front door.

"Mrs B and Anthony!" hissed Sophie. "Quick! Give me the Shadow Files!"

Sam passed the book to her and she slipped it into the big inside pocket of her waistcoat.

"We're back!" called Mrs Benton. Mrs B did all the cooking and cleaning at Keeper's Cottage, and when Sophie and Anthony's parents were away for work, she helped Grandpa look after the twins.

"PHWEEEEEEEEE!" There was the sound of a football whistle blowing as Anthony, Sophie's twin brother, followed Mrs B in.

Mrs B came through to the kitchen. "Hello, duckies."

Anthony was right behind Mrs B. He had thick blond hair like Sophie and the same sporty, athletic build. "Oh, great!" he groaned loudly, as he looked at Sam. "You're here!"

"If you don't like it then you could just go away again," Sophie suggested. "For good."

"Ha ha." Anthony pulled a face at her. "There really should be a law about being as unfunny as you!"

"And there should be a law about being as dumb as you!" retorted Sophie.

"PHWEEEEEEEEE!" Anthony blew his

whistle at her.

"Fetch it, Nigel!" Sophie pointed to Anthony. With a squawk Nigel flew off her shoulder and plucked the whistle out of Anthony's hand.

"Hey!" Anthony spluttered, as Nigel gave it to Sophie.

She twirled it round in her fingers. "Oops, looks like you lost your whistle!"

"Give it back!" said Anthony, angrily.

Sophie folded her arms. "Gonna make me?"

"Now, now, twins," said Mrs B. She plucked the whistle out of Sophie's fingers and gave it back to Anthony, who put it in his jeans pocket. "That will do. No more blowing that whistle in the house though," she warned him. "Now go and take your football boots off and then move your night things into Sophie's room. You'll be

sleeping in there for the next few nights."

"WHAT?" Sophie and Anthony both gave her looks of complete horror.

Mrs B nodded. "The decorator who's painting your room didn't have time to finish everything today, Anthony. He'll be back on Monday and will finish then."

Anthony gaped. "I can't share with Sophie!"

"No way!" Sophie said, agreeing with Anthony for about the first time in her life. "And anyway, Sam's staying over tonight, Mrs B!"

"So, you can all share together." Mrs B beamed at them all. "It'll be fun!"

Fun! Sophie blinked. Sharing a bedroom with Anthony would be about as much fun as sharing with a Swamp Boggle!

"Oh, come on, Mrs B," Anthony pleaded. "What about the spare room? Can't I sleep in there?"

"No, I'm sorry, Anthony-duckie, but I'm storing some things for my niece up there. There are boxes all over the bed."

"So, I'll move them or… or sleep on the floor!" Anthony said. "Anything would be better than

sharing with those two weirdos."

"Don't say things like that, Anthony. I'm afraid you just can't stay in the spare room," Mrs B said, patiently. "There's valuable china in those boxes. In fact, I don't want any of you going up there at all." She glanced down at them all. "You'll have a lovely time tonight, just think of it like being at a party!"

Anthony stomped out of the kitchen.

"Oh, great. Just kill me now!" Sophie muttered.

3

The Uninvited Guest

Sophie and Sam walked slowly upstairs. "I can't believe we've got to share with Anthony," said Sophie.

"Maybe your grandpa will say we don't have to," said Sam hopefully. "Mrs B goes home after supper, doesn't she? Well, why don't we ask your grandpa if we can sleep in the

The Bat Sprites

lounge or on the landing or…"

"In the bath?" suggested Sophie. Anywhere would be better than sharing with Anthony! "You're right. We'll ask Grandpa later." She lowered her voice. "Should we look for the gem now? The spare room has got floorboards instead of carpet. I know Mrs B said we mustn't go up there, but we have to check!"

Sam nodded, and they crept up the second flight of stairs to the spare room in the attic. There was a walk-in cupboard built into the far side of the room, and the double bed was covered with boxes saying FRAGILE.

"Is there a creaky floorboard in here?" wondered Sophie. She walked around the wooden floor, listening hard. "No, nothing," she sighed.

"Maybe it isn't in here after all," said Sam.

"There'll be floorboards under the carpet in the other rooms."

"Great, I can just imagine Mrs B's face if I start ripping up the carpet!" giggled Sophie as they left the room.

They reached the bottom of the staircase just as Mrs B appeared with an armload of towels. She frowned as she put them in the bathroom. "Have you two been in the spare room?"

"No," Sophie lied. "We… we were just playing on the staircase."

"Good. You know I don't want to see any of you going up there."

As Mrs B went downstairs again, Sam and Sophie headed for Sophie's room. Suddenly two balls of paper flew out of Anthony's doorway. One hit Sophie on the head and one hit Sam.

"Ten points for the geek. Ten points for the freak!" Anthony crowed as he jumped out.

Sophie leaped at him, but he immediately pulled out a can from behind his back.

"Come any closer and I'll fire!"

Sophie saw that it was a can of foam filler that the decorator had been using. She'd watched him that morning as he'd squirted it into the cracks in the walls – the foam had frozen almost instantly into a stiff pale-green mass, which he'd then filed away and smoothed down.

Anthony advanced with the can held out in front of him. "I'm going to sleep with this in my hand tonight, and if you come anywhere near me I'll get you with it."

"Yeah, like we'd want to come near you!" Sam retorted. Sophie watched her brother warily. She knew he wouldn't hesitate to squirt her with the green foam, and he had a very accurate aim.

Anthony smirked and ran down the stairs.

"There's absolutely no way I can cope with him all night!" grumbled Sophie. They went into her room, and she gritted her teeth as she saw Anthony's clothes dumped on her bed.

Sam nodded. "Maybe we can ask your grandpa if we can camp in the garden?"

Seeing that her window was open, Sophie went to close it. It was almost dark outside now.

As she reached for the handle, she paused. A tingling had started in her toes and power was surging up through her body.

"Sam, my Guardian powers!" she said in alarm. "There must be a shadow creature nearby!" Whenever Sophie was near a shadow creature, the Guardian magic made her super-strong and super-fast.

"Maybe there's one in the garden," said Sam, joining her at the window.

Suddenly they both yelled and ducked as a black bat flew straight at them.

It was as big as a squirrel with wide, outstretched wings, and it was making strange squeaking, clicking noises. It swooped over their heads, and Sophie swung round just in time to see it change into a figure as tall as she was, with grey, furry skin and red eyes gleaming in its evil-looking face. It smelt horrible, like rotting food and bad eggs.

Sophie jumped into a fighting stance: hands up, one leg slightly in front of the other. She didn't feel scared – not with the Guardian powers flowing through her. "Who are you? What are you doing here?" she demanded.

"I want the gem. The key has shown us that it's here," the bat creature snarled. "And I'm going to get it!"

Sophie raised her eyebrows. "Oh, you are, are you?"

"Don't toy with me!" The creature showed its pointed fangs. "Where is it, little girl?"

Sam winced. "That's so not a good thing to call her."

Before he'd finished speaking, Sophie was attacking the bat with a front snap kick, lifting her right leg up and lashing out with her foot. It caught the creature square in the chest. "Ooh, sorry, the little girl must have tripped," snapped Sophie.

The bat shrieked and grabbed at Sophie's foot with its long fingers, catching her ankle. Sophie saw its fangs flash down and managed to turn her fall into a back flip, yanking her foot free. She landed nimbly, dodging as the creature swung at her, and then kicked her leg out in a circle, her shin thwacking into the back of its legs. It fell forwards with a hiss.

"Oopsy, tripped again!" she grinned.

"Yeah, and take that!" Sam grabbed the bin and threw it over the creature's head. Balls of

paper and apple cores rained out.

"Argh! Get this thing off me! Get it off!" The bat's voice was muffled as it staggered around, bumping into the bed and bookshelves. Its screeches and squeals echoed back until finally it toppled over and the bin fell off its head.

"You'll pay for that!" it screeched as it leapt at Sophie, yellow fangs bared. She snatched up a metal trophy she'd won for tae kwon do and thwacked it hard on its head.

The creature keeled over and lay still.

For a moment, there was silence. Sophie and Sam both stared at the bat's grey, furry body lying on the floor.

"Is it… is it… dead?" breathed Sam.

Sophie swallowed and bent over the creature. Its chest still seemed to be moving. She poked

47

it with her foot, but it didn't stir. "I think I just knocked it out."

"Sophie!" Mrs B called up the stairs. "It sounds like there's a herd of elephants in your bedroom. What are you doing?"

Sophie ran to the door. "Nothing!" she called. She turned to Sam. "Quick! We've got to get rid of it!"

"Great idea! How? It's as big as we are!"

"You must be doing something," Mrs B shouted. They heard her footsteps coming up the stairs.

Sophie looked wildly at Sam. "Oh, no! What do we do now?"

Sam's eyes were wide. "Panic!"

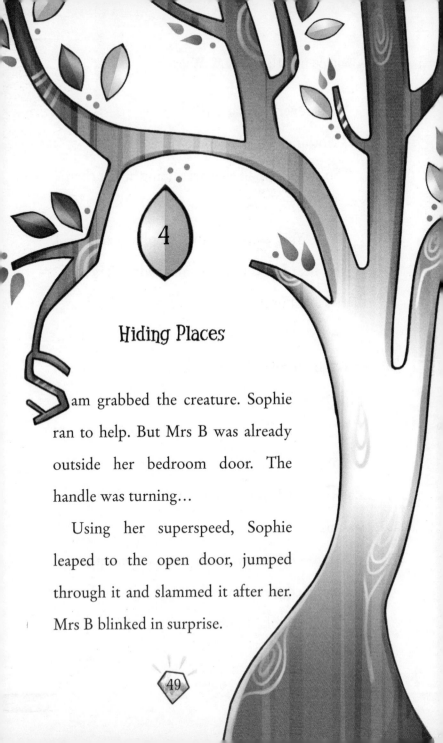

4

Hiding Places

Sam grabbed the creature. Sophie ran to help. But Mrs B was already outside her bedroom door. The handle was turning…

Using her superspeed, Sophie leaped to the open door, jumped through it and slammed it after her. Mrs B blinked in surprise.

49

"Whatever's going on?"

"Nothing!" Sophie smiled brightly.

"So what was all that screaming about then?" Mrs B reached for the door handle.

"No! You can't go in!" Sophie exclaimed, as she heard a thump from inside. "There's... there's a bat in there."

"A bat?" Mrs B stared. "Did it come in through the window? Well, let me in. I don't mind bats. I'll catch it and — "

"I didn't mean a bat!" gabbled Sophie. "I meant you can't go in because Sam's... Sam's... making a rat! Yes, he's sitting behind the door making a rat."

Mrs B's eyes narrowed. "Sam's making a rat," she repeated disbelievingly.

"For school," Sophie went on. "We're doing

the Middle Ages, and there were lots of rats then, spreading the plague. We had to make one for homework, and we were pretending it was real – that's what all the crashing was about. Right, Sam?" She shouted through the door. "You're making a rat for your school project!"

"Sophie." Mrs B's voice grew strict. "Let me past, please. There is something going on in your room and I want to see what it is."

"Sam!" Sophie called desperately. "Mrs B wants to see that rat you've been making!"

"Er... OK," Sam replied. "Just a second!" There was another thump, a few seconds of silence and then Sam opened the door.

"Hi, Mrs B." He held up a piece of rolled-up paper from Sophie's bin. He'd hastily drawn on two eyes, two ears and some whiskers. "This...

this is my rat. Eek eek!" He waggled it around.

Mrs B frowned, sniffed the air suspiciously and walked into the room. Sophie looked around frantically. Whatever had Sam done with the creature?

A dark foot fell out from under her bed.

Sophie gave a squeak of alarm. Leaping across the room, she pushed the foot back under the

bed before Mrs B could see. The housekeeper turned round.

"Sophie? Are you all right?"

"Yes. Fine! Absolutely, wonderfully fine!" gulped Sophie.

"Well, everything seems OK in here," said Mrs B, looking like she couldn't quite believe it.

Sam held the rat up. "It's like Sophie said. I'm just doing my school project."

Mrs B shook her head. "I'd better go and finish off supper then," she said.

Sophie felt the creature's foot flop against her own foot again and quickly kicked it under the bed as Mrs B went out. Sam shut the door and they both collapsed on the floor.

"That was close!" Sophie said.

"I almost died when its foot flopped out!" agreed Sam. "Imagine if she'd seen it."

Sophie didn't want to imagine it! "What are we going to do now?" She peered under the bed. The creature lay there, its red eyes shut, but its long fangs and wings making it looking eerily like a vampire. "We've got to get rid of it!"

"But how?" said Sam.

"Push it out of the window?" suggested Sophie.

"What if Mrs B sees it in the garden?" pointed out Sam. "And what if it wakes up and tries to get back in?"

Sophie groaned. "We need Grandpa. Look, let's put it somewhere safe and ring Grandpa on his mobile. He'll help us work out what to do."

"But where do we put it?" protested Sam. "We can't leave it in here! Anthony could come in at any second."

Sophie had an idea. "The spare room! It's the only place no one will go. It can go in the big cupboard up there and I can lock it in. It'll only take me a few seconds to stick it in the cupboard and come back down. You can keep guard. Yell if Mrs B or Anthony starts to come up the stairs and I'll whizz down super-fast."

Sam looked doubtful, but he nodded. "OK."

Sophie pulled the creature out from under the bed. The foul smell coming off it was like toilets and old milk mixed together, and seemed to be growing stronger by the second. "Ew! It really stinks!"

Sam made a face. "Yuck, I can really smell it

now too." He went to the door. "Looks like the coast's clear."

"Operation Dracula begins!" said Sophie, wrinkling her nose and throwing the bat over her shoulders. Its fur felt greasy to the touch, and its fangs were dangerously close to her skin.

She raced up the stairs to the spare room at superspeed. Opening the big, built-in cupboard she pushed the creature inside, propping it against the wall. She tried to shut the door, but its body slumped sideways, forcing it open. Argh! Sophie tried to shove it back inside again, but without success. Then to her horror she heard Sam's warning yell. Someone was coming! What now?

Looking around, she saw a chest at the end of the bed. Grabbing the creature again, she quickly lifted the lid and dumped it inside.

"Just practising my singing, Mrs B!" she heard Sam say in a very loud voice. "No, I don't know what that smell is either."

Mrs B said something Sophie couldn't catch.

"You think it's coming from the SPARE ROOM?" bellowed Sam. "No way!"

Eek! Mrs B was on her way up! Sophie had no time to do anything other than pull the lid of the chest shut and then jump back into the wardrobe herself. She closed the door and sat in the dark, her heart pounding as she heard Mrs B come into the room.

"Yes, it definitely seems to be coming from up here," she heard the housekeeper say.

Sophie edged into one corner of the wardrobe in case Mrs B opened the door. There was a creak and she felt something move under her legs.

She reached down and pressed. The floorboard wobbled! A creaking floorboard! Could it be... could it be...?

Moving as silently as she could, Sophie gently prised up the loose floorboard. There was a space underneath. She reached into it and felt her fingers close on a hard, round gem. She pulled it out and saw it glittering with a turquoise glow. The final shadow gem! She'd found it!

"Well, there's nothing that's obviously causing a smell up here," said Mrs B's voice. "But I think I'll open the window." Sophie heard her unlatching the sloping attic windows. "Now, I must get back to that bolognese sauce before it burns. Come downstairs please, Sam. I don't want anyone up here."

There were sounds of footsteps leaving. Sophie listened hard. Had Mrs B definitely gone?

"Sophie?" she heard Sam's whisper. He'd crept back up the stairs. "Where are you?"

"In here!" Sophie opened the door and scrambled out. "And look!" She held up the glittering turquoise gem, grinning in delight.

Sam gave a whoop. "You found the final gem! So now we've got them all! We—"

"Ssh!" Sophie said quickly, as she heard a suspicious thump from inside the trunk – but it was too late.

BANG! The lid of the chest fell open and the creature sprang out. "You have the gem!" it screeched, flying at her.

Sophie threw herself to one side, the gem tight in her hand. She leapt up as the bat rushed at her again. "Give me that gem!" Its voice rose. Just then a piercing noise split the air as the smoke alarm went off in the kitchen. Mrs B had obviously not reached her bolognese in time.

The high-pitched sound screamed through the whole house. Sophie jumped into the air, kicking out with her left foot. But to her astonishment the bat had blundered away, shrieking and covering its ears with its hands. It began to crash about from side to side, smashing blindly into things.

Sophie landed and stared. "What's happening to it?"

"I don't know!" Sam jumped out of the way as the creature almost bumped into him. It saw the open window and with a last desperate squeal dived out, wings flapping.

It had gone.

Sophie and Sam looked at each other. The smoke detector stopped. "Quick, we'd better get downstairs!" Sophie could feel her powers fading now the shadow creature had gone. She grabbed Sam's hand and they raced back into her room.

"Well, that was weird," said Sophie. "But at least it went away."

Sam's face was anxious. "But now it knows you've got the gems – it heard me say we've got all of them! It's bound to come back."

"Maybe with some friends," worried Sophie.

"That wouldn't be good," said Sam.

Sophie gulped as icy fingers trickled down her spine. "No, not good at all!"

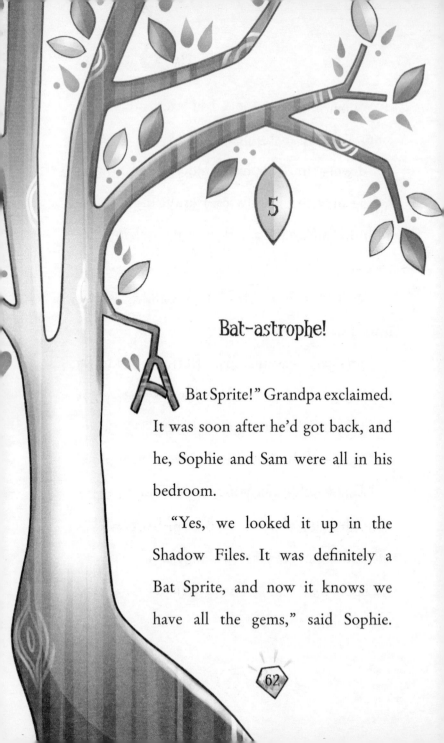

Bat-astrophe!

A Bat Sprite!" Grandpa exclaimed. It was soon after he'd got back, and he, Sophie and Sam were all in his bedroom.

"Yes, we looked it up in the Shadow Files. It was definitely a Bat Sprite, and now it knows we have all the gems," said Sophie.

"What should we do?"

Grandpa paced around. "We need to hide the gems somewhere they won't be found. I don't know where yet – I need to think this through. For the moment, let's keep all the windows closed and get ready to fend off an attack if one comes. Did the Shadow Files say anything about how to defeat Bat Sprites?"

"Not really." Sam handed him the book opened to the right page. "All it says is they live in a big group, and like to sleep in the day and are awake at night."

Sophie looked over Grandpa's shoulder at the hand-drawn picture of the Bat Sprite. As well as the note about the bats' sleeping habits, the word ECHOLOCATION was written in capitals and underlined.

"Hmmm," said Grandpa, seeing it too. He stroked his chin. "Echolocation."

"Echo-what?" asked Sophie, puzzled.

"Echo-location,' replied Grandpa. "Normal bats use it to help them fly in the dark. Their eyesight isn't great, so they send out sounds and then work out what's around them by listening

to the echoes that come back. Maybe Bat Sprites do the same." Grandpa sighed and closed the

book. "Which is interesting, but it would be more helpful to have notes on how to defeat the creatures! Right, go and check all the windows are closed and then get anything ready that you think might be useful in a fight. If the word spreads through the woods that we have all the gems here, we may have other visitors – not just the Bat Sprites. I'm going to go tell Mrs B she can go home for the night. I'll walk her home to make sure she's safe from the shadow creatures – you two will be OK for a few minutes, won't you?"

"Yes, of course," said Sophie, hoping she sounded more brave than she felt. "And what about Anthony?"

"I'll say he can play on the PlayStation all evening; that'll keep him out of the way and occupied," said Grandpa. He fixed them with a worried look. "Get moving!"

Sophie and Sam quickly checked all the windows and drew the curtains shut. Downstairs they could hear Grandpa seeing Mrs B out of the house and offering to walk her to her cottage. The PlayStation was on in the lounge and nothing made Anthony happier than being allowed to play on it for hours, so hopefully he was out of the way for the night.

Sophie got her rucksack out from under her bed and then she and Sam started going around the house filling it with all the things they'd used to fight shadow creatures in the past – the torch they'd shone on the Fog Boggarts who hated bright light; a bag of salt because salt had melted the Icicle Imps; a can of starch they'd used to

66

harden the skins of the Swamp Boggles, so that Sophie's kicks would hurt them. As she took the starch from the cupboard she also took a tin of lemon furniture polish, because Spider Gnomes hated the smell of lemon. She grabbed a can of bug spray too, just in case.

"We've fought some pretty horrible creatures, haven't we?" she said to Sam, as they made their way back to her room. "Which do you think were the scariest?"

"Definitely the Spider Gnomes." Sam shuddered. "Just think of their horrible big grey bodies and eight legs. Though the Icicle Imps were pretty freaky too – remember that one, Snowy, who Anthony thought was a white squirrel and tried to keep as a cute little pet? He was nuts!"

Sophie giggled, but the word 'cute' reminded her of something. "The Swamp Boggles didn't like the Fluffy, did they? We'd better get it out too, just in case." She took the pink fluffy toy from a drawer in her cupboard. It had enormous blue eyes and long curled eyelashes.

As she pressed its start button, its eyelashes fluttered. "Wanna cuddle, Mama?" it said in a dalek-like voice. Sophie grimaced, but put the Fluffy in her rucksack.

Just then the door opened. She swung round and saw Anthony standing there, armed with the can of foam filler.

"I thought you were playing on the PlayStation," she said.

"I am," said Anthony. "I just wanted to get

my hoodie. It's cold in the lounge." Holding the can like a weapon to keep Sophie back, Anthony picked his hoodie off Sophie's bed. Then he sniffed and looked around. "It smells really gross in here. Is it you?" he said to Sam.

Sam folded his arms over his chest. "No."

"What is it then?" Anthony wrinkled his nose. "This place stinks like a baboon's pants! Let's open a window."

"No!" Sam and Sophie cried, both jumping to their feet. "Don't open the window!" went on Sophie. "Don't even go near the window."

Anthony raised his eyebrows. "You know, you seriously should take pills for your weirdness. Why shouldn't I open the window?"

"Just... just don't. There could be something out there."

Anthony chortled. "Aw, is ickle Sophie scared of the bogeymen out in the dark?" He reached for the window handle.

Sophie felt her powers surge through her. A shadow creature must be near! "Stop!" she shouted.

She leaped for Anthony just as he pushed the window open and called, "Come on, Mr Bogeyman. Come and get... WAAAA!"

Five Bat Sprites swooped in with ear-splitting screeches. They soared over Anthony, Sophie and Sam's heads and landed behind them, instantly changing to their full size.

Anthony's eyes bulged. "V... v... vampires!" he gibbered.

The five sprites filled Sophie's bedroom, blocking the way to the door with their black,

scaly wings. The leader stepped forwards, his red eyes on Sophie. "Give me the gems!" he screeched.

"Let me see…? Hmmm – no!" Sophie leaped into action, spinning round and lashing out with her feet.

THUNK! Her heel connected with the Bat Sprite's head. He staggered backwards, knocking two of the other Bat Sprites with him. But there were still two left standing. With a squeal, one of them flew straight at Sophie. She jumped on to the bed, gave a bounce and somersaulted over his head. Landing behind him, she kicked him over before he realised where she was.

"Soph! Watch out!" Sam shouted as the fifth Bat Sprite leapt at her. Sam grabbed the can of

filler foam Anthony had dropped and sprayed it at the sprite. It covered the top of its head, filling its ears with green foam that turned stiff and hard.

The sprite staggered, giving Sophie a chance to spin round and kick it over. It rolled on the floor, pawing at its ears and squealing. "Argh, get that stuff off my ears! Get it off!"

The other four had already leaped to their feet again. "Grab the boy!" the leader screeched.

One of the other Bat Sprites pounced on Anthony, who shouted in terror. Sophie stared as the Bat Sprite scooped her brother up and flew out through the window!

"No!" she shouted.

The Bat Sprite flew high up in the air, even higher than the roof of the house. He held

Anthony under the shoulders, dangling him above the ground.

"The gems – or the boy drops!" hissed the sprite.

Sophie looked wildly from Anthony to the leader of the sprites.

Far above, Anthony kicked his legs. "Sophie! Give them the stupid things they want. And you, please please put me down!" he begged.

"My pleasure!" screeched the Bat Sprite holding him – and he let go.

Sophie gasped, as Anthony screamed and started to plummet. Then the Bat Sprite swooped down and caught him again. "Whoops! Slipped!" He squealed with high-pitched laughter.

"He'll slip some more unless you give us the gems." The leader held out his long fingers.

"Give them to me."

Sophie hesitated, her heart thudding. What could she do? She couldn't let them drop Anthony. He'd be seriously hurt, or worse, if he fell from that height!

"Give them to me or the boy goes!" snapped the sprite again.

Sophie swallowed and glanced at Sam. He looked as helpless as she felt. Slowly, she reached under her t-shirt and pulled out the leather pouch that she had in her purse belt. She clutched it in her palm for a moment, her throat dry.

"Here," she whispered, holding it out.

With a shriek of delight the leader snatched the gems. "We've got them!" He soared out of the window. The other three grabbed the sprite with the green foam in his ears and followed. As

they all flew away, the last sprite threw Anthony back inside Sophie's room.

Cackling triumphantly, the five Bat Sprites changed into regular bats and zoomed away. "We've got the gems!" they screeched. "The gateway can be opened. Every creature in the shadow realm will come through!"

6

Shadow Magic

Sophie and Sam stood rooted to the spot, almost unable to believe what had just happened. All the gems had gone!

Anthony scrambled to his feet. "What... what were those things?"

Sophie's bedroom door opened and Grandpa looked in. "Is everything all right? I heard noises when I got back after taking Mrs B home. What's—"

"There were monsters here, Grandpa! Like vampires!" Anthony gabbled.

"Bat Sprites," explained Sam grimly.

Grandpa's eyes widened. "Are the gems still safe?"

"No. They took them," Sophie whispered.

"Took them!" Striding over to her with a scowl, Grandpa grabbed her by the shoulders. "The shadow creatures have got the gems?"

Sophie nodded, tears prickling her eyes. She almost never cried, but she couldn't help it now.

Sam stepped forwards quickly. "It wasn't Sophie's fault. She fought really hard, but there were five of them. One grabbed Anthony and took him out of the window and he was going

to drop him. Sophie had to give them the gems."

Sophie looked at Grandpa desperately. "I couldn't let them hurt Anthony, Grandpa!"

She saw Grandpa's shoulders sag and the anger leave his face. "Of course you couldn't. You did the right thing, child. OK!" His tone changed, it became commanding. "We have an emergency on our hands. We must go to the gateway and stop them opening it – no matter what it takes."

Sophie grabbed up her rucksack. "Let's go!"

Sam nodded determinedly. "We'll get the gems back, and the key too!"

"Wait!" Anthony wailed. "Where are you all going? I don't understand what's going on. What are Bat Sprites?"

"We're going to have to tell him what's happening, Grandpa," Sophie said, looking at

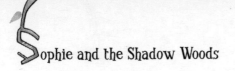

her bewildered brother.

"We can't!" spluttered Grandpa.

"We have to," Sophie insisted. "We can't pretend nothing's happened."

Grandpa sighed reluctantly. "OK. Listen, Anthony, there are things going on – big, bad dangerous things. Sophie's right, we can't pretend you didn't just see the Bat Sprites, and anyway, it isn't safe to leave you here on your own. You'll have to come with us to stop the shadow creatures opening the gateway – and that means you'll have to help us fight."

"Fight those bat things?" Anthony said weakly.

"Yes, and probably other far scarier creatures. You have to be brave. I know it's a lot to get your head around, and I promise I'll tell you everything, but we have to focus on getting the

gems back." Grandpa turned to Sophie and Sam. "You two get moving! Go to my room. Under my bed you'll find another rucksack and a case with useful things in. Take what you can and meet me by the back door in two minutes sharp." They hesitated. "Go!" he urged. "If I know Ug, he's going to want to gloat for a while before he opens that gate, but we must get there as quickly as we can!"

Sophie and Sam raced down the corridor. Under Grandpa's bed they found two nets, some rope, another very bright torch, a penknife, a golf club and a hockey stick. They threw everything into the rucksack, with the handles of the golf club and hockey stick poking out through the zip at the top.

"Let's take the rest of that can of filler foam too," said Sophie, as they ran back to her bedroom. "That Bat Sprite really didn't seem to like it."

"It was weird, wasn't it?" agreed Sam. "It went kind of nuts. A bit like the Bat Sprite did earlier when the smoke alarm went off."

"Maybe they're allergic to foam and loud noises?" suggested Sophie.

"Mmm," said Sam doubtfully. "Maybe."

"Well, whatever the reason, let's take the foam – we might need it." Sophie threw the can in the rucksack and took a deep breath. "Ready to go?"

Sam nodded. "You bet."

Looking at his eager face, Sophie suddenly felt very glad that he was coming with her. "Just think, if you'd never found out about me being the Guardian you'd probably be at home right now. Do you wish…" She stopped.

"What? That I was?" Sam finished for her. He pretended to think. "So, I could be at home watching TV, eating crisps or I could be about to try and save the world?" He grinned at her. "I say, let's save the world. Bring it on!"

They ran downstairs. Grandpa and Anthony were in the kitchen. Anthony looked pale. "He knows everything now," Grandpa said.

"You're... you're a superhero," Anthony faltered, as they handed Grandpa his rucksack. "I mean, how's that possible? My freaky sister's a superhero?" He looked at Sam. "And you're her side kick?" He shook his head. "This is like... against nature."

"Whatever," said Sophie. All she could think about was getting to the gateway and stopping Ug from opening the gate. The words from the Shadow Files rang in her head: One Guardian will never close the gate. Ug mustn't be allowed to open it, no matter what! She opened the back door. "Come on, let's go!"

But as Sam ran out he stopped. "Look!" They

followed his gaze to the woods.

Sophie felt her stomach somersault. The Shadow Woods never looked inviting, but now they were even more menacing than usual. The trees had twisted into strange shapes, their leaves turning black and limp, their branches looking like skeletons' arms in the darkness. Weird shapes darted here and there through the shadows.

"What's happened?" Sophie gasped.

Sam groaned. "Of course! I read about this in the Shadow Files. If the gems are all taken into the woods then they start creating shadow magic. The Shadow Woods are the passing place between the Shadow Realm and the human world. As the shadow magic in them increases, they'll become more like the Shadow Realm and less like our world."

Sophie shoved her fear away and lifted her chin. "Well, whatever's happening – we're going in!"

Hurrying across the back garden, she vaulted over the fence. As her feet touched down on the grass of the Shadow Woods, she felt the Guardian magic surging through her, stronger than ever before! The gems might be firing up the shadow magic, but they seemed to be doing something to her too!

Sam jumped over the fence and joined her. Anthony was holding back, staring at the woods in fright. "Maybe I'll just wait here…"

"No!" snapped Grandpa, pulling him over the fence. "You've heard what we have to do, and you've got the blood of generations of Guardians running through your veins. Show some courage, boy!"

"This way!" called Sophie, heading into the trees.

The others followed. Sophie had been to the clearing where the gateway was before, but now the woods were different. Trees seemed to close across the path as they were walking along it, forcing them to fight their way through. Twice Anthony landed in the middle of a blackberry bush. "I don't like this," he moaned.

"Sssh!" said Sophie. She was sure she could hear a low cackling in the trees ahead. "There's something nearby." She peered into the thick, soupy darkness. "It could be any of the shadow creatures!"

"I just heard a noise!" Sam gulped and looked to the left. "Like a laugh – a snigger…"

"I heard something too!" interrupted Anthony, pointing to the right. He pulled the hockey stick out of Grandpa's rucksack and held it up anxiously. "Kind of high-pitched and squeaky."

"And there's something behind us," said Grandpa, looking over his shoulder. "Squelching footsteps! I think it's a Swamp Boggle."

Sophie's heart began to beat faster as she heard another hissing cackle, closer now – and then

the cracking of leg joints. That wasn't a Swamp Boggle. Her breath caught in her throat. "We're surrounded!"

A cackling scream came from the trees in front of her. "ATTACK!"

A giant, spider-like creature swung towards them on a web of rope. A Spider Gnome! The next second Sophie saw an army of fluffy white Icicle Imps leaping out of the trees at them like evil furry snowballs. A dripping Swamp Boggle with a gaping mouth, green-brown skin and long bony fingers came running at them from behind.

"This time we'll get you, Guardian!" screamed the Spider Gnome. He let go of the web rope and plunged through the air straight at her, his sharp teeth glinting…

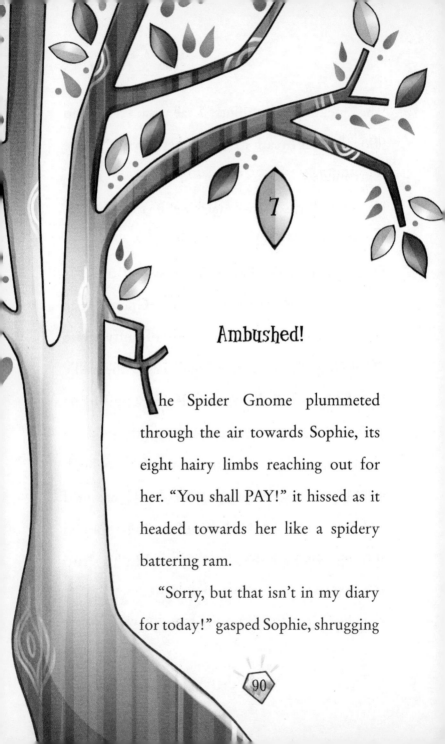

Ambushed!

The Spider Gnome plummeted through the air towards Sophie, its eight hairy limbs reaching out for her. "You shall PAY!" it hissed as it headed towards her like a spidery battering ram.

"Sorry, but that isn't in my diary for today!" gasped Sophie, shrugging

off her rucksack and flinging herself over in two quick back flips. As the Spider Gnome thumped into the ground where she'd been standing, she attacked with a volley of kicks, sending it flying. It crashed into a tree with a horrible cracking noise, and howled with rage.

Sophie folded her arms. "OK, let's get this straight, bug-face. I'm going to the gateway and no one's going to stop me. So, if I were you, I'd just swing on back to my web and stay there like a good little spider."

Hearing yells behind her, Sophie glanced around.

Grandpa was holding off the Swamp Boggle, but his blows were sinking harmlessly into the boggle's soggy body. While he kicked and punched, Sam and Anthony stood back to back

surrounded by fluffy Icicle Imps who looked
like cute white squirrels.

"There are hundred of creatures like Snowy!"
Anthony cried in astonishment. "Look at them
all…" He gasped as the imps' fangs all snapped
out in unison. "WHOA!"

The leading imp sprang at Sam. "Attack!" it

squealed, landing on his head and gripping his hair. "Quake in your shoes, human! Fear for your life!" It swung upside down to look into his face.

"Snowy!" burst out Sam, recognising the leader of the Icicle Imps.

"My Snowy?" cried Anthony, his face lighting up. "Snowy, come to Daddy!" Dropping the stick, he pulled Snowy from Sam's head. "OW!" he shouted, as Snowy sank razor-sharp fangs into his hand. "You little freak!"

Anthony flung the imp away. It landed with a bounce and leapt to its feet. "Prepare to feel my fury, miserable humans!" it squeaked.

"They don't really make very good pets," said Sam. "Not unless you like fluffy snowballs with fangs attacking you."

"Well, they're picking on the wrong person here!" Anthony grabbed the hockey stick off the floor, as Snowy sprang at his face. He hit the imp as if it was a hockey ball. Snowy soared away into the trees. "Goal!" yelled Anthony as if he were in a hockey match. The other imps leaped at him and Sam, but Anthony kept swinging and hitting, sending them flying into the trees one after the other.

"Howzat!" Anthony shouted, punching the air.

Meanwhile, the Spider Gnome had staggered to its feet. Two of its legs were hanging uselessly.

"You're really not listening, are you?" sighed Sophie as the Spider Gnome lunged again. "Oh, well, if you really want to get hurt..." She spun round in a blur, kicking out high and sending the Spider Gnome flying backwards again. As it

94

crashed down, she ran to her rucksack, reached inside and flung the packet of salt at Sam. "Here! Use this!"

"Thanks!" Sam missed and the packet burst open on the ground. He grabbed up handfuls of salt and started chucking it at the imps; they shrieked as they began to melt.

Sophie pulled out the Fluffy next. "Grandpa! Catch!"

The Swamp Boggle gave a burbling hiss as the pink cuddly toy flew through the air towards him, its tiny arms outstretched. "No!" the boggle yelled. "Not the Fluffy!"

Grandpa leapt up, caught the Fluffy and pressed its button.

"Fluffy wanna wee-wee!" the Fluffy squealed.

The Swamp Boggle shouted as spots started

sprouting all over its body. It backed off in terror as Grandpa advanced, waving the cuddly toy.

"Fluffy wuv yoo! Do yoo wuv Fluffy?" Grandpa said.

"AARRRGH!" screamed the boggle, running off into the trees.

Sophie grinned, but then her smile died as she heard a hiss. She swung round just in time to see the Spider Gnome right behind her. Before she had time to move, it jumped, his six uninjured legs slamming her to the ground.

Her breath was knocked out of her. The Spider Gnome threw its head back with a triumphant hiss. "Now, I get to eat you, Guardian!"

"Get off her, you spidery creep!" Sam yelled. Sophie caught sight of him running to the rucksack and pulling out two spray cans. With

his fingers on the triggers, he charged at the Spider Gnome. Lemon furniture polish and bug spray hissed out in white clouds.

The Spider Gnome screamed as the two sprays hit it at the same time, blasting it off of Sophie. Its body jerked and writhed, legs twitching as the bug spray started to work. With a shriek of anger, the Spider Gnome scuttled away into the trees.

"Are you OK, Sophie?" Grandpa demanded.

She got to her feet. "Sure," she said, slightly shakily. "There's nothing I like better than almost being a spider snack! Thanks for rescuing me, Sam," she added gratefully.

"No problem. Thanks for chucking the salt to me."

"Did you see me go!" crowed Anthony, throwing the hockey stick in the air and catching it. "Those mutant snowball suckers didn't stand a chance." He rubbed his hands together, his green eyes gleaming. "What do we fight next?"

"Whatever we meet." Sophie looked grimly into the shadows. "Come on!"

As they raced through the dark, looming trees, Sophie could sense shadow creatures watching them from every direction, but none attacked. The paths twisted and turned. The Guardian power throbbed within her, pulling her in the right direction. It was like every cell in her body was urging her towards the gateway, telling her to hurry.

Finally they found themselves on a path she was sure she recognised. "Look, Grandpa," she whispered, pointing ahead. "Isn't that the clearing where the gateway is?"

He nodded. "Quiet everyone," he said to Sam and Anthony. "We don't know what's waiting for us in there."

"Bat Sprites and Ink Cap Goblins, I bet," said Sophie, as she breathed in the unmistakable stench of the Bat Sprites mixed with the rotting-compost odour of Ink Cap Goblins. "Wait here!"

With a burst of superspeed, she ran to the edge of the trees and peered through the branches into the clearing. What she saw made her feel as though her heart might stop.

At least fifty Bat Sprites ringed the clearing, their wings folded around themselves, their red eyes glittering. In the centre was the pale figure of King Ug with his three Ink Cap Goblin servants. In one hand King Ug held the key. In the other he held the bag of gems. A look of triumph shone in his beady eyes.

"King Ug said he would do it!" he crowed. "King Ug really is the cleverest, sneakiest goblin of all time. I said I would open the gateway and now I shall! Every creature in the shadow realm will come!"

Sophie dashed back to the others. "Quick!

There's about fifty Bat Sprites there, and Ug's about to open the gateway!"

Sam and Anthony leaped forwards.

"Wait!" Grandpa snapped out, stopping them. "We can't just go storming in. We need a plan."

Sophie stamped in frustration. "We haven't time, Grandpa!"

"Have you discovered the Bat Sprites' weakness yet?" asked Grandpa. "There must be some way they can be defeated. What can we do?"

"How about I hit them so hard they fall over?" suggested Sophie, her feet edging down the path.

"Um – I might have an idea," said Sam cautiously. "I've been thinking about the way that Bat Sprite flew away when the smoke alarm went off, and how the one who got the foam in his ears seemed to go nuts. Do you remember, in the Shadow Files it said—"

"There isn't time for this!" broke in Sophie. "We have to go now! Plan if you want, but I'm going to the clearing." And without waiting for an answer, she set off at a run.

8

Unlocking the Gateway

atch and wonder as the magic of the key is released!" King Ug shouted gleefully to the other shadow creatures. He had the key in one hand and the turquoise gem in the other. He chucked the bag with the other gems in it to Flaky Face.

Sophie burst into the clearing

with Grandpa, Sam and Anthony hot on her
heels. "Or they can watch and wonder as I kick
your crumbly butt!" she shouted to King Ug.

There was a riot of hisses and snarls as the
shadow creatures saw who it was.

"Your fun stops here!" Sophie halted in front
of King Ug and put her hands on her hips.

"Playtime's over, Uggy-boy. I want that key and those gems back, and I want them now!"

Grandpa, Sam and Anthony turned and faced the Bat Sprites, raising their weapons. Anthony had the hockey stick and Sam had grabbed the golf club from Grandpa's rucksack. Grandpa took up a tae kwon do fighting stance.

Ug puffed out his chest. "So, Guardian! We meet again!"

"We do," said Sophie, "and unless you give me that key in the next five seconds I'm going to get you like I did at our last meeting."

"Now, let me see...' Ug pretended to think. "Sorry, but the answer's 'no'." He smirked at the other shadow creatures and twirled the key in his hand. "I think I'll hang on to the key. In fact, I think I'll open the gateway with it while you watch! Get her!" he yelled.

The Bat Sprites swooped forwards, squealing and shrieking.

Grandpa and Sophie spun round, lashing out with their feet and knocking the first wave of Bat Sprites backwards. Sam and Anthony yelled, thwacking at any others who came within range.

Sophie flipped and somersaulted, knocking one Bat Sprite into another.

But there were just too many sprites for them to fight. Sophie saw one of them grab the hockey stick out of Anthony's hands and fling it into the trees. Two of them lifted him up, cackling, and four flew at Grandpa. Then they grabbed Sam too. Sophie was the only one left free!

She used every bit of her superspeed and superstrength, but there were so many Bat Sprites and just one of her. As she landed after a spin, she felt one of the sprites grab her ponytail, then another two grabbed her shoulders and four more dived at her legs. She struggled and kicked desperately. "Let me go!"

But it was no use. Even with her superstrength, she was overpowered. While Grandpa, Sam and

107

Anthony were dragged to one side, she was pulled into the centre of the clearing, face to face with King Ug.

"Well!" he gloated triumphantly. "So you're going to 'get' me are you, Guardian?"

"You're going to be so sorry for this!" Sophie tried to tear her arms free.

"Silence her!" Ug snapped.

The next instant, one of the Ink Cap Goblins was tying a piece of grimy cloth around her face and Sophie couldn't say another word. "Mmf!" she spluttered.

Ug peered at her. "Now then, I wonder how pretty you'll be after a bit of goblin-goo." He lifted one black splodgy arm up and held it over Sophie. "So many parts of you to drip on. Where do I start?"

Sophie flinched and pulled back as hard as she could. The Bat Sprites pushed her forwards, laughing with a hissing sound.

Ug chortled. "You know, I think I shall save my fun until later. First you shall watch me open the gateway and see the hoardes of shadow creatures come through!"

He held up the key. Sophie's mind raced. What could she do? *Think, think!* she shouted in her head.

Slowly, Ug brought the key and the gem together. The gem slotted into the hole in the centre of the key's handle with a quiet click and turquoise light poured out. The Bat Sprites and Ink Cap Goblins cheered and whooped.

"Behold! The magic key!" cried Ug triumphantly, holding the glowing key aloft.

Sophie's eyes widened. Behind Ug the gateway had shimmered into life, appearing out of nowhere as a solid silver metal.

Ug strutted towards it. There was a keyhole under the handle. He swung round, smirking. "Are you watching, Guardian?"

"Mmf! Mmf!" Sophie struggled harder, but the Bat Sprites held on fast, their fingers gripping her arms like pincers.

Ug put the key in the lock. As he did so, silver light flashed across the metal. He turned the key and Sophie, Grandpa and Sam held their breath in horror.

"All unlocked!" Ug taunted Sophie, pulling the key out and waving it at her without opening the gate. "I thought you said something about stopping me, Guardian?"

Sophie stared in horror, helpless as Ug put his fingers on the handle. At the same moment, she heard a kerfuffle behind her. She managed to swing round enough to see Sam breaking free from the sprites who'd been holding him. "The whistle! Have you still got that football whistle on you, Anthony?" he yelled.

"Yeah!" Anthony wrenched a hand free and pulled the whistle from his pocket. "Here!" He chucked it towards Sam. Sam ducked nimbly around the Bat Sprites and scooped it up as it fell to the ground.

Sophie felt several Bat Sprites loosen their

grip on her in their confusion. She didn't know what Sam was doing, but she seized her chance. Throwing herself forwards, she tore free, somersaulted over and bounced to her feet. WHAM! Bringing her foot up and round, she slammed it into Ug's chest.

"WHAAAA!" he shouted, staggering backwards.

The Bat Sprites leaped at her. Sophie ripped the rag from her mouth and fought them off.

Sam lifted the whistle and blew a long, piercing note.

PHWEEEEEEEEEEEEEEE!

Instantly, all the Bat Sprites reeled back. They shook their heads and blinked their eyes. Sophie stared in surprise. Not one of them was trying to attack her, and they had stopped holding on to Grandpa and Anthony too!

"What are you lot doing?" shrieked Ug.

"Can't see!" howled a Bat Sprite above the noise of the whistle, staggering into a tree trunk.

"Can't see anything!" said another.

"Echolocation!" Sam gasped, as he paused

to take a breath. "The Shadow Files weren't just making a note about how Bat Sprites navigate, they were telling us what to do! Bat Sprites have poor eyesight and usually they make noises and listen to the echoes to work out where things are. If you make a high-pitched noise they can't hear anything. It's like turning them blind and it drives them crazy!"

He blew again, even harder. Ug gave a furious yell and charged at him, but Sophie was ready; she raced in between them and lashed out. Ug skidded to a stop and retreated to the gate. Meanwhile, the Bat Sprites were wailing and flapping away into the trees, desperate to get far from the noise.

"Very clever," Ug snarled at Sophie as the Bat Sprites fled the clearing. "But you shall not stop me, Guardian! The gate is unlocked. It shall be opened!"

"No!" Sophie leaped forwards, as he put his hand on the gateway. But she was too late. With one quick move, Ug had started to open the gate! A dark light came rushing out and immediately there was the sound of thousands of shadow creatures shouting and cheering from the other side.

Enormous tentacles snaked around the door, waving in the air, pushing the gate open.

"Welcome, my shadow friends!" crowed Ug. "Welcome to the human world!"

9

Expect the Unexpected

Sophie reached Ug and threw herself at him. He stumbled forwards. Time seemed to slow as Sophie saw the key jerk from Ug's hand and fall through the gateway into the Shadow Realm.

"The key!" she and Ug both yelled.

They leaped through the gateway after it. As Sophie jumped into the Shadow Realm, she felt an iciness freezing her skin. The world inside the gateway was dark and shadowy and smelled even worse than the Bat Sprites. She got the impression of thousands of creatures charging towards her through the gloom, and saw a giant grey octopus-like monster waving its suckered tentacles.

But most of all she saw the key. It lay on the muddy ground, glowing with the turquoise gem in its handle. Ug was already on his knees reaching for it, but Sophie, with her superspeed, was faster. She dived past him, grabbed the key and leaped back through the gateway into the human world.

"Stop!" she heard Ug shriek from inside the

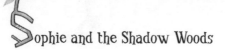

Shadow Realm, as Sophie frantically tried to push the gate shut. She knew the prophecy had said she wouldn't be able to, but she had to try anyway! She forced her weight against it.

"Push!" Grandpa exclaimed, joining her on her left side.

"Push!" Sam yelled, joining her on her right.

The door moved inch by inch. But now Sophie could feel the army of creatures pushing from the other side. For a moment she thought she saw a dark shadow slither out through the crack. She felt a lurch of fear and pushed even harder and then she felt Anthony's hands thud on to the wood beside Sam's. "PUSH!" he shouted. The door suddenly slammed shut. Sophie didn't hesitate. Thrusting the key back into the lock, she turned it. The door locked with a click.

The handle rattled frantically, but the door wouldn't open. From the other side, Ug yelled with frustration and anger. "You can't do this to me, you stupid child!" he shrieked. "Open the gate, open it!"

Taking the key out, Sophie pulled the gem

from its handle. The glow left it and the gateway vanished. Dimly, she heard Ug cry "Noooo!" … and then his voice faded to nothing.

They all stood gaping, hardly able to believe it.

"We… we did it!" stammered Sophie. "But how? The Shadow Files said the gateway couldn't be shut by the Guardian once it was opened."

"It must have been wrong," said Grandpa.

"Is this the moment to say 'phew!'?" said Sam shakily.

"I feel weird." Anthony looked down at his legs and arms. "Really weird. Kind of trembly…"

"It's stress," said Grandpa.

"Dizzy," said Anthony, blinking. "Tingly…"

"We really did it!" shouted Sophie, relief

fading and exhilaration rushing through her. "I've got the key. The doorway's shut. Ug's gone!" She grabbed Sam and they jumped up and down, laughing. "It was brilliant of you, Sam, to think of using the whistle like that to get rid of the Bat Sprites!"

"Yes, very clever indeed," agreed Grandpa with a smile. "As always, Sam."

Sam went red. "It was nothing. Just one of those ideas."

"Yeah, those genius ideas that you have all the time," said Sophie, nudging him. She looked around the clearing. It was so quiet now. All the shadow creatures had gone…

No, not all, she realised, as she spotted Flaky Face in the shadows, escaping with the bag of remaining gems.

With a yell she charged – but before she could reach him, Anthony had overtaken her! He jumped into the air kicking out with his left foot and then his right. Flaky Face howled as he slammed into a tree trunk and slithered down it.

Anthony grabbed the gems from his hand.

Scrabbling to his feet, Flaky Face fled away into the trees.

Slowly, Anthony turned, looking dazed. "What did I just do?"

"You… you attacked a shadow creature," said Sophie faintly, staring at him.

"Just like the Guardian would," said Grandpa slowly.

"But I'm not the Guardian," said Anthony.

For a moment they all stared at each other and then Grandpa shook his head. "Oh, my goodness…" he said. "Oh, my… no!"

"What?" cried Sophie and Anthony together.

Grandpa looked from one to the other. "There must always be a Guardian in the world," he breathed.

Sophie frowned. "Yes, and I'm here!"

Grandpa hit his head with his hands. "But you weren't! Don't you see? You went out of this world, into the Shadow Realm, to get the key! And while you were in a different world there was no Guardian here in this world."

Sophie's eyes widened. "So, you mean another Guardian was created…"

"Your nearest blood relative," said Grandpa, nodding.

They both swung round to look at Anthony.

"Oh, no!" Sophie whispered. "He's the Guardian too!"

"So, let me get this straight," said Anthony for about the hundredth time, as they all walked back through the woods towards Keeper's Cottage a little while later. "You're saying I'm

the Guardian as well as you."

"Yep. It's you and me." Sophie swallowed. "Which is why the gate shut when you came to help push – the Shadow Files were right. One Guardian couldn't do it, but two could." Her heart sank into her trainers as she spoke. Was she really going to have to fight shadow creatures with Anthony?

She could tell Sam liked the idea about as much as she did. "Maybe there's a way of turning him back?" he said to Grandpa. "I mean, now Sophie's back in this world, couldn't we deactivate Anthony or something?"

"I don't think it works like that," sighed Grandpa.

"And, if you think you're going to deactivate me then think again, geek-brain! This is awesome! I've got superpowers. No way am I changing back," said Anthony, spinning round and kicking out at a tree. "Yee-ha!"

Sam and Sophie exchanged looks. "Nightmare," she said helplessly to him.

"Times a million," agreed Sam.

Grandpa shook his head, as they walked out of the woods. "I don't know what to say. First, you come along, Sophie – the only girl Guardian there's ever been – and now, also for the first time ever, we have two Guardians. What's going to happen next?" He rolled his eyes. "Actually, don't answer that. I don't think I want to know!"

They climbed the fence and Sophie turned to look at the woods. Now the gems had left the woods, the trees were changing back to how they'd been before. Gradually the branches

untwisted, the leaves grew again and the shadows lost a little of their eeriness. As Sophie watched them it started to sink into her brain that even though there was the shock of Anthony becoming a Guardian too, they had actually won the fight!

"We really did it, didn't we?" She looked down at the key in her hand. "We got the key back – and the gems. We shut the gateway and Ug's on the other side. We saved the day, Grandpa!"

Grandpa smiled and squeezed her shoulder. "You're right. We did and we should certainly celebrate. How about a takeaway pizza party?"

"Definitely!" said Sophie and Sam.

"What's that noise?" Anthony said suddenly.

"What noise?" Grandpa frowned.

"It was like a laugh – a chuckle? Coming from

the trees." Anthony pointed.

They all listened, but there was just silence.

"You must have imagined it," said Sophie. "Now, what was that you were saying about pizza, Grandpa?"

"Oh, I think a couple of giant-sized ones with lots of toppings, a massive bottle of lemonade and a bucket of cookie-flavoured ice cream is just what we need," said Grandpa. "Then afterwards, Anthony, I can tell you all about the Shadow Files and show you how to keep the notes in them up to date."

"You mean there's writing? You never said anything about writing!" Anthony exclaimed in alarm.

"Ah, well, you see, Anthony," Grandpa put his arm over Anthony's shoulders, "being the

Guardian is a position of great responsibility. You must prepare and practise, work day and night. When I was a young Guardian…"

Sophie shook her head as she watched them go into the house, Grandpa still talking. "How is this going to work out?" she said to Sam.

"I have absolutely no idea." Sam looked at her. "But for now I think we should do what your grandpa said – eat pizza and celebrate!"

Sophie high-fived him. "Bring it on!"

As their hands met, happiness surged through her. The shadow creatures had been defeated, the gateway was locked, Ug had gone and the key and the gems were back in their safe-keeping. There was no danger any more.

"Come on," she said. "It's time to party!"

Grinning at each other, she and Sam ran into the house.

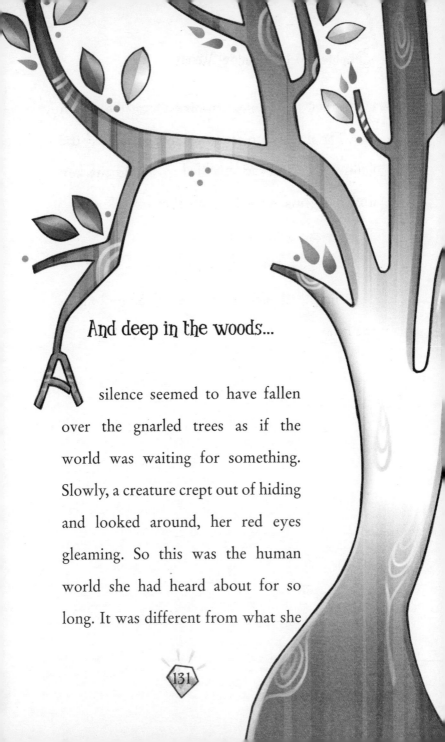

And deep in the woods...

silence seemed to have fallen over the gnarled trees as if the world was waiting for something. Slowly, a creature crept out of hiding and looked around, her red eyes gleaming. So this was the human world she had heard about for so long. It was different from what she

131

had expected but no matter. She would soon make it hers. Fire flickered around her long yellow nails and she chuckled softly. At last, her time had come!

THE
SHADOW
FILES

King Cobra Sprites

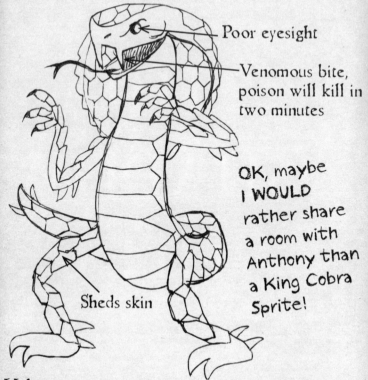

Poor eyesight

Venomous bite, poison will kill in two minutes

OK, maybe **I WOULD** rather share a room with Anthony than a King Cobra Sprite!

Sheds skin

Habitat
King Cobra Sprites coil around the base of tree stumps and grab their prey as it passes.

General note
Like all sprites, snake sprites are spiteful and vicious. Be very careful and always attack first.

Hidden near where the Guardian sleeps

Search for a board that doth creak

Lift it up and you shall see

A gem shining beautifully.

If the goblin king joins gem and key
And opens the door then soon you'll see
There's no point fighting, it's too late
One guardian will never close the gate.

Shadow Magic

Shadow Magic is magic that seeps into the human world from the Shadow Realm. It is believed that if all six hidden shadow gems are taken into the Shadow Woods, shadow magic will be created. The Shadow Woods is a passing place between the Shadow Realm and the human world. It has been suggested that as the shadow magic in them increases, they will become more like the Shadow Realm and less like the human world.

Given this, it is vitally important all six gems are NEVER taken into the woods.

This is what it looks like if they do enter the woods...

SERIOUSLY CREEPY!!!

You can say that again!

Bat Sprites

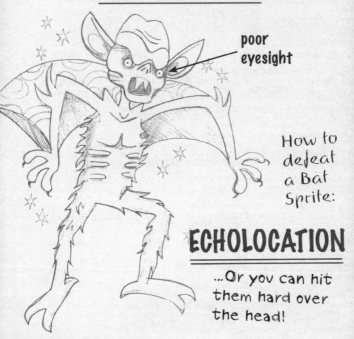

poor eyesight

How to defeat a Bat Sprite:

ECHOLOCATION

...Or you can hit them hard over the head!

Bat Sprites' Habits:

Bat Sprites roost in large groups. They are nocturnal, generally sleeping in the day and hunting at night.

Diet:

Bats, owls, foxes: possibly have cannibal tendencies? Need to verify.

What animal is best at cricket?

A bat.

What did one Bat Sprite say to another?

Let's hang round together.

Surviving an ambush

For those who want to discover how best to fight an Icicle Imp, consult the EXPERT i.e. Anthony Smith!

1. Pick up stick

2. Wait for imp to jump at you

3. Hit as hard as you can — though this won't work if you're as rubbish with a hockey stick as Sam, the geek-brain.

Ignore Anthony, he's just visiting this plan

The Gateway

Do NOT go through!!

I'm afraid these notes are simply not good enough. Re-do them, please.

NOTES

COLLECT ALL OF SOPHIE'S AMAZING ADVENTURES!

"Do you have what it takes to be the NEXT GUARDIAN?"

Prove your worth for a chance to win AWESOME prizes!
It's simple and fun!

◆ Read the *Sophie and the Shadow Woods* series
Answer three questions about each book
Pass a stage, collect a gem, enter for great prizes/freebies
Pass SIX stages and get entered into the grand prize draw!

Stage Six – THE FINAL STAGE

Answer these simple questions about *The Bat Sprites*:

1. Where did Sophie and Sam hide the Bat Sprite?
2. What colour was the last gem?
3. Who became Guardian when Sophie entered the Shadow Realm?

Got the answers? Go to:

www.sophieandtheshadowwoods.com

You can find Stage One in *The Goblin King*, Stage Two in *The Swamp Boggles* and Stage Three in *The Spider Gnomes*, Stage Four in *The Fog Boggarts* and Stage Five in *The Icicle Imps*.

Good Luck!